Annie Pitts, Artichoke

Annie Pitts, Artichoke

Diane de Groat

SIMON & SCHUSTER BOOKS FOR YOUNG READERS
Published by Simon & Schuster
New York   London   Toronto   Sydney   Tokyo   Singapore

SIMON & SCHUSTER BOOKS FOR YOUNG READERS
Simon & Schuster Building, Rockefeller Center
1230 Avenue of the Americas, New York, New York 10020
Copyright © 1992 by Diane deGroat
All rights reserved including the right of reproduction
in whole or in part in any form.
SIMON & SCHUSTER BOOKS FOR YOUNG READERS
is a trademark of Simon & Schuster.
Designed by Vicki Kalajian
The text of this book is set in 13 pt. Goudy Old Style.
The illustrations were done in pencil.
Manufactured in the United States of America.

10 9 8 7 6 5 4 3 2 1

Library of Congress Cataloging-in-Publication Data
deGroat, Diane. Annie Pitts, artichoke / by Diane deGroat.
p.   cm.   Summary: When Annie and her third grade class
put on a play about nutrition, it has more surprises
than the teacher expected. [1. Schools—Fiction.
2. Nutrition—Fiction. 3. Plays—Fiction.] I. Title.
PZ7.D3639An 1992 [E]—dc20 91-33558 CIP
ISBN: 0-671-75910-8

Acknowledgments

I would like to mention the terrific people who modeled for
the illustrations in this book. Laura Murray posed
for the pictures of Annie. Laura's mother,
Margaret, was perfect for the role of her mother,
because she is. She also appears as the grandmother.
Anthony Buete was Matthew, and Connie Schwartz
(a real teacher!) played the role of Miss Goshengepfeffer.
Incidentally, Connie would like everyone to
know that she is not really that fat. And, finally,
a thank-you to the staff at the Roaring Brook School
in Chappaqua, New York for letting me wander
through their halls with my camera.
—D.d.

Contents

1

Miss G. and Me

As I stared out the classroom window, I watched a black dog crossing the empty playground. He stopped to sprinkle on the monkey bars. I would have to remember not to climb on that side of the monkey bars at recess. I would also have to remember to tell everyone else not to climb on that side. Everyone except Matthew, that is. I would tell him after he did.

When the dog wandered off, I stared at my reflection in the glass. I tilted my head and practiced smiling. I practiced smiling every chance I got because someday I was going to be a television star and I would have to smile a lot for the camera.

I would also have to cry a lot. I made a frown in the glass and tried to think of something sad. I thought about the time Bambi's mother died. I was about to cry, really, but then I saw Matthew's reflection behind mine. He was making silly faces. It's so hard to be a serious actress when someone is making silly faces at you.

Matthew's reflection suddenly disappeared, because something large came between us. It was Miss Goshengepfeffer. "Earth to Annie Pitts!" she said.

I jumped and said, "Sorry, Miss G."

Miss Goshengepfeffer was nice enough to let us call her Miss G., but she was not nice enough to let us daydream in class.

Miss G. returned to the front of the room. "As I was saying," she said, looking my way, "the play will be for your parents and for the rest of the school, too. We'll write it together, and everyone will have a part."

Play? Did I, Annie Pitts, future star, hear that magic word, *play*? My best friend, Sara, and I used to put on plays in her backyard. We charged kids a quarter to see one, which was really a bargain. I mean, a video game costs a quarter, and it can be over in less than a minute. Our plays went on for hours.

Since Sara moved away over the summer, I haven't had a chance to do any serious acting, so I suddenly paid very close attention to what Miss G. was saying. "We can start working on the play at the end of our new science unit," she said. "But first I'd like to tell you about the class trip that's coming up."

I wanted to hear more about the play, but everyone else wanted to hear about the trip. Last year her third graders went to a baseball game. I heard that Miss G. ate ten hot dogs! I believed it, because Miss G. is . . . you know . . . large.

Thomas raised his hand. "Are we going to a baseball game?"

Miss G. said, "No, we're not going to a baseball game, but we are going someplace interesting. And you've probably been there before."

"This summer I went on a trip to Disney World," Thomas said. "Is the trip to Disney World?"

Disney World? I hoped we could go to Disney World! I've always wanted to be a Mouseketeer. Maybe I could try out for a part when we go on the trip. I was thinking about which name to use for the show, Tiffany or Brooke, while Miss G. was writing something on the board: SUPERMARKET.

Supermarket? What has that got to do with Disney World, I wondered. And then I realized: We weren't going to Disney World. No Mickey Mouse Club. No chance to be a TV star. We were going food shopping! That was not my idea of a class trip.

I guess I wasn't the only one who thought so. Thomas asked, "Why are we taking a trip to the supermarket? I've been there plenty of times."

I found that hard to believe, because Thomas's

family had a housekeeper who did all the shopping for them. I couldn't imagine Thomas, or even Thomas's mother, in the supermarket trying to decide between the floral- or the pine-scented room spray.

"The supermarket can be very interesting," Miss G. said. "Our new science unit is about nutrition. We're going to do a play about it, but first we'll learn about making healthy choices in our diet. And all the different foods we'll be discussing can be found right in our local supermarket."

Miss G. wrote NUTRITION on the board. I didn't copy it on the paper in front of me when she asked us to. Instead, I wrote M-I-C-K-E-Y M-O-U-S-E.

"Now, who can name some good foods?" Miss G. asked, her chalk hand ready to write.

Marsha said, "Ooh, ooh," and waved her arm. Obviously, Marsha-Miss-Pick-Me-Pick-Me wasn't very upset about not going to Disney World.

"Chocolate!" she said. "Chocolate is good."

"Chocolate is very good," Miss G. said. "And so are doughnuts and cookies. But they are not foods that are good for us. We need to eat foods that contain . . . protein." She wrote the word on the board. "Meat, fish, chicken, and eggs are all sources of protein. Beans and nuts have it, too."

I looked over at Matthew, looking over at me, making nutty faces. If nuts had protein, then Matthew must have more protein than anyone else in the class.

4

Miss G. drew a huge circle on the board. She drew a fork on one side and a knife and spoon on the other. Then, for some reason, she drew a guitar right in the middle of the circle.

"Now we need some vegetables, a dairy product, and either a cereal or pasta. That will give us something from each of the four food groups," she said.

She looked at me and said, "Annie, what vegetable shall we put on our plate?"

I was still staring at the guitar. "Plate?" I said.

"Here, next to the chicken," she said. "I guess I'm not a very good artist." She wrote the word CHICKEN on the guitar. I mean, on the chicken.

"Well, Annie," she continued. "What vegetables would you like?"

"I don't like vegetables," I said very matter-of-factly. And that was true. I always left them on my plate. But I could probably learn to like them in Disney World.

Miss G. was not giving up so easily. "Annie," she said. "We can all learn to eat right even if there are certain foods we don't like."

Before I could stop myself, I said, "Don't you eat right, Miss G.? I mean . . . how come you're so . . . so . . ."

Some kids giggled. Marsha-Miss-So-Polite gave me a look that said, "How *could* you?"

But Miss G. wasn't mad. She said, "You're right, Annie. I don't always eat right, as you can see." She

patted her hip. "I just love sweets: cake, ice cream, cookies . . . chocolate!" She sighed a little before going on. "But I've started a new diet this year, and I'm going to eat only the foods that are good for me. I should set an example for my students."

We all agreed that Miss G. should lose some weight. And we would help her. Matthew said that he would check her desk each morning to make sure that she wasn't sneaking in doughnuts. Thomas suggested that she take karate lessons. Marsha suggested that I keep my mouth shut.

2

The Trip to You-know-where

On the day of the trip, Miss G. gave us a talk about proper trip behavior. I already knew how to act in a supermarket, but maybe some kids didn't. I once saw a little boy throw a tantrum when his mother wouldn't buy him candy. Maybe Miss G. was afraid one of us might do the same. Maybe she thought it would be me.

As we headed out the door, Miss G. said, "Don't forget your nutrition charts. You have to find examples from each of the four food groups." My chart had M-I-C-K-E-Y M-O-U-S-E written across the top. But that didn't change the fact that this trip was going to be pretty B-O-R-I-N-G.

When we lined up in front of the school, five cars were already waiting at the curb. Because my mother works, she couldn't volunteer to drive us. My grandma, who takes care of me during the day, doesn't know how to drive. Otherwise, she'd probably have volunteered, because she's a person who really likes to shop. She even has a sweatshirt that says, "Shop till you drop."

I was hoping to go in Miss G.'s car. I could just see myself sitting next to her in the front seat. I would use my most polite, grown-up voice when we laughed and talked. Maybe she'd tell me all about how she never ate vegetables when she was little, either, although it was hard to imagine Miss G. ever being little!

Marsha's mother was driving the first car, so Marsha got to go with that group. The line moved forward, and before I knew it, I was sitting next to Matthew in the backseat of his mother's car.

"Wait!" I said. "I'm supposed to go with Miss G.!"

But Matthew's mother was busy checking seat belts and locking doors. I was trapped. She pulled the car away from the curb and started down the road to you-know-where, and I was sitting next to you-know-who. It was going to be a you-know-what kind of day.

Matthew was not happy about sitting next to me, either. I could guess that, because the first thing he said was, "Hey, Fish-face! Don't get any cooties on me!" Matthew has called me Fish-face ever since we were in kindergarten. Grandma said it was because he liked me. I think it was because I called him a doody-head.

The five-minute drive felt like an hour. I had to make sure that my leg didn't touch Matthew's, and that took a lot of concentration. Finally, we reached Shopper's Supreme, the neighborhood supermarket, which was about as exciting as a dead cat. Although I guess a dead cat could be an exciting thing if it was your pet and it died and you were really upset and you had a funeral for it.

"Please stay in line, and watch for cars!" Miss G. shouted as we walked across the parking lot.

My group followed Matthew's mother into the store. We all gathered by a corner booth that had a sign, MANAGER, on it. A bald man in a white shirt with the sleeves rolled up waited until we were all quiet. He looked very familiar.

"Good morning, boys and girls!" he said loudly. "And welcome to Shopper's Supreme — the only store you need for all your shopping needs."

Now I knew who he was. He was Hank, the Shopper's Supreme man in the TV commercial. I, Annie Pitts, was standing in the same room with a famous person! I've always wanted to meet a famous person. I raised my hand.

"Are you really Hank, the Shopper's Supreme man on TV?" I asked.

"I certainly am, young lady," he answered. "And are you one of my loyal customers?"

"Oh yes," I lied. "I do all my shopping in your store." Maybe if I sounded as if I really meant it, Hank would want me to be in one of his commercials. I would rather be in a regular TV show, but being in a commercial would be great, too—as long as it wasn't for underpants or something like that. That would be *so* embarrassing.

"Now, there's a satisfied customer," Hank said, pointing to me. "How would you like to be my helper?"

Would I! He actually asked *me*. He didn't ask Marsha-Miss-Teacher's-Pet-Who-Gets-Picked-All-the-Time. He asked Annie Pitts. I smiled and said in my best actresslike voice, "It would be your pleasure to have me."

Hank laughed and asked me to come forward. I stood next to him and smiled out at the class. Through my smiley teeth I tried to say, so only Hank could hear, "Just so you know, I don't do underwear commercials."

Hank gave me a funny look and handed me a huge poster to hold. On it was a diagram of the whole store. This was supposed to help us find all the different kinds of food.

Unfortunately, I was holding the poster in front of my face, so I couldn't see any of the diagram, but I did

11

see Marsha taking lots of notes. She was probably trying to impress Hank so that she could be in one of his commercials, too. She could be so obvious sometimes.

When he was finished, Hank wished us all good luck and asked us to remind our parents that Shopper's Supreme was the only store they needed for all their shopping needs. I was left holding the poster, while the rest of the class headed for the aisles.

"Thank you, miss," Hank said, taking the poster. "You'd better catch up with the others." He picked up some important-looking papers and rushed past me. I guess he would talk to me later about my television career.

3

Lettuce Begin

Miss G. had told us earlier to stay with our groups, so I looked for Susan, Thomas, and Matthew. I found them in the fruits-and-vegetables aisle with Matthew's mother. They were running around, busily writing down things as if it was fun or something. I looked at my chart and wrote APPLES under the fruit column. This was just too exciting for words.

Miss G. saw me. "There you are, Annie," she said. "I told the others that I'm giving a star for each correct answer. We're trying to see who can get the most stars."

Miss G. made it sound as if the person with the most stars would get a prize or something, like maybe the *starring* role in the school play! That must be it! I'd have to do some fast catching up.

Miss G. walked down the aisle saying, "Try to be creative. I'd like to see some unusual choices. The most interesting names will get two stars."

I checked my chart. Apples were definitely not a two-star fruit. I looked around for something more interesting. I found persimmon and guava. Maybe this would be fun after all.

I rushed across the aisle to the vegetables. As I said before, they were not my favorite kind of food, but maybe there were some unusual veggies worth two stars. I had to weave my way around a lot of shopping carts.

The store was suddenly very crowded, and I got trapped against the display case, completely surrounded by shopping carts. Behind me was a huge pile of lettuce. I never thought of any vegetable as being very interesting, but lettuce had to be the dullest of them all—that is, until someone takes a head from the bottom of the pile and they all start to roll. Which is exactly what Matthew did. I suddenly found myself being attacked by iceberg lettuce!

Matthew's mother helped me up and apologized to the vegetable man, who was trying to stop the last of the rolling lettuce. I would have offered to help, but I had more important work to do. I rushed through the cases, adding to my list jicama, arugula, fennel, rutabaga, and taro—all worth at least three stars!

15

As my group made its way to the dairy aisle, I kept my eyes open for Hank, in case he wanted to talk to me about any ideas I had for our commercial. I didn't see him anywhere, so I worked on my chart.

The dairy aisle was easy. I found weird stuff like feta cheese and soybean milk. As I waited for everyone else to finish, I practiced modeling with a container of strawberry yogurt. I held it up and smiled, pretending there was a camera in front of me. I picked up another yogurt—blueberry—and held it up also. I tried to see how long I could stand perfectly still and smile at the same time.

I was doing a really professional job, I thought, until I noticed that people were looking at me. That was okay. I would have to get used to that if I was going to be in commercials. Then I saw that they really were looking at Matthew, who was standing behind me and making faces.

His elbow suddenly hit my hand, and I dropped one of the yogurts. It squished out all over the floor and onto my shoes. There is nothing more disgusting than having blueberry yogurt squished all over your white sneakers.

Fortunately, Hank wasn't around to see the mess I had made. Unfortunately, Miss G. was. She mumbled something about early retirement and handed me some tissues so that I could clean up myself.

I hoped she would still let me be in the play after this. I would have to keep away from Matthew from now on so I wouldn't get into any more trouble!

Just then an announcement came over the loud speaker: "Cleanup in the dairy aisle . . ." It was Hank's voice.

As I shuffled my blueberry sneakers over to the meat department, I wondered if Hank actually saw me drop the yogurt or if one of his workers reported that there was just a general mess on the floor, without mentioning the eight-year-old redhead who made it.

Suddenly, I found myself face-to-face with fish—dozens of fish lying on a bed of ice. Actually, the fish were very interesting. They were shiny and scaly and had eyes that followed you when you walked past. Of course Matthew couldn't resist saying, "Hey, Fish-face! See any relatives here?"

And then it happened. Some strange person inside of me made me pick up one of the dead fish by the tail. My arm no longer belonged to me. It flung the fish straight at Matthew and smacked him in the face.

Of course I had nothing to do with it. It was that stranger inside of me. So you can imagine my surprise when Matthew started yelling at me. He didn't call me Fish-face, either. He used a word I had never heard before. It couldn't have been a very nice one, though, because his mother grabbed him by the collar and took him off to the side for a talk.

Miss G. remained somewhat calm. I thought that was very cool. She apologized to Hank, who, by the

way, had witnessed the whole ugly scene. That was not cool. He politely asked us to leave his store; and before we knew it, we were being escorted to the exit.

I never found out what happened to the fish. It was last seen stretched out on the green linoleum of Shopper's Supreme. But its fate couldn't have been any worse than what was about to happen to me. Miss G. told me that I was to ride back with her group. And I don't think she wanted to talk about her childhood eating habits, either.

4

The Story
of Horace Tuttle

I always thought it would be special to ride in a teacher's car. The fact that I was about to get a lecture made it not-so-special. It could have been, if only I hadn't flung that fish.

Miss G. cleared her throat as she pulled out of the parking lot. I sank lower into my seat and pretended I was admiring the treetops that whizzed past. If she didn't say something soon, I figured I would have to start talking about the weather. But I didn't have to wait very long.

"Annie," she said. "I do understand that Matthew teases you and makes you angry—but you must try to control yourself. If people took it upon themselves to solve their problems the way you just did, the world would be in a sorry state."

I tried to imagine everyone in the whole world tossing fish around, and I had to agree with her. Things could get really messy. And smelly. My hand still smelled a little fishy. I wondered if Matthew's face smelled fishy, too.

Miss G. continued. "The rest of the class seems to be able to work nicely together. I just wish you could be a little less independent and follow directions like everyone else." She looked at me hopefully and said, "Can you give it a try, Annie?"

"Yes, Miss G.," I said. I really meant it, too.

Miss G. gave me a little smile, and I smiled back. For the rest of the ride we were silent, but the kids in the backseat were still laughing and fooling around. I guess they didn't think it was so special to be riding in a teacher's car. I know I would never forget it.

When we reached the school, everyone rushed for the classroom, but Miss G. called me back. Uh-oh, I thought. Now that we're alone, she's really going to let me have it. But what she said surprised me.

"You know, Annie," she began. "When I was your age, there was a boy in my class who teased me so much that I finally had to do something. Something bad. I knew I wasn't a bad person, but something inside of me had to do something bad to Horace Tuttle."

My jaw dropped. "What did you do to Horace Tuttle?" I dared to ask.

"I glued his math book shut," she said quite casually.

I gasped. My own teacher had done what she always told us not to do. We were not to treat a book unkindly. If we made a pencil mark in our books, we were being "unkind." Imagine globbing glue between the pages. That would be like murdering it! I stared at her as if she were suddenly from another planet.

Miss G. went on. "Even though I paid for the book, my teacher made it clear that she was disappointed in me. Maybe that's why I'm such a 'clean book' fanatic today!"

Miss G. chuckled a little, but I didn't think it was funny. I hoped she wasn't disappointed in me. Maybe I should offer to pay for the fish. Or maybe I could buy some special shampoo that would get the smell out of Matthew's hair. Finally, I decided that I should just try harder to stay out of trouble.

Once we were back in the classroom, Miss G. acted just like she always did. She was very good at pretending that she was a normal teacher and not an ex-book murderer. She could probably be an actress someday if she really wanted. I would be sure to suggest it to her when I got a chance. I could even help her practice smiling.

We spent the rest of the afternoon reviewing proper trip behavior. Again. My guess was that the play would be canceled because some of us acted so poorly. That's no play and no commercial. I could see that my acting career was off to a pretty slow start!

I was very surprised when Miss G. announced that the play would go on as planned. "Maybe we shouldn't," she said, "but this is the last chance for all of you to show me that you really can work together." She was looking at Matthew and me when she said that.

I was very good for the rest of the day, which was about ten more minutes. I didn't even laugh when Matthew tripped on his way to the board. The rest of the poorly behaved class did, but not me. I sat perfectly still with my hands folded on my desk. I was so good for so long that I almost exploded by the time the bell rang.

When I got home, I told my grandma all about the trip and how I got into trouble. I didn't tell her about Horace Tuttle, but she smiled whenever I mentioned Matthew's name.

"I remember a boy who always teased me when I was in school," she said.

"Was his name Horace Tuttle by any chance?" I asked.

"No, I called him Silly Willy."

"What did you do about Silly Willy?" I asked.

"I married him." She laughed. "Your grandpa William wouldn't leave me alone until I did!"

My grandpa died last year; but all the time I knew

him, he always teased my grandma. He would put a flower behind his back, and she'd have to guess which hand it was in before he gave it to her. Silly stuff like that.

All of this wasn't helping me much. I would have to deal with Matthew in my own way, but I would have to think about that later. Right now I wanted to concentrate on the school play. Miss G. had asked us to think up some ideas for it.

I thought of a really good idea. I could be a TV chef who shows viewers how to make fancy stuff like wedding cakes. Only I would make healthy stuff like whole wheat wedding cakes. The rest of the class would be the camera crew, except for Marsha-Miss-Never-Touch-Dirt. I would make her clean up the kitchen after me.

The next day we discussed our ideas in class. Miss G. listed three of our best ideas on the board, including mine about the TV chef. I was sure my idea was the best. It was far superior to Matthew's idea about killer tomatoes eating people and Marsha's idea about a cook finding a magic kettle.

We raised our hands to vote for our favorite. To my surprise, Marsha-Miss-I-Won-I-Won got the most votes. Things went downhill from there.

Miss G. listed all the parts on the board so that the kids could choose their roles. Due to the unfortunate fish incident at Shopper's Supreme, Miss G. said that Matthew and I would have to choose our parts last.

But I couldn't complain. I was just happy she let us be in the play at all.

Of course Marsha-the-Wonderful got the leading role as the cook, because the story was her idea. One by one, everyone picked his part. The junk foods were very popular. Susan got the part of the Twinkie, and the new kid, Elan, chose the chocolate bar. Some of the other junk foods were ice cream, peppermint candy, and my own personal favorite, jelly beans. Patty took that part. I was *so* jealous.

When there were no more junk-food parts left, the class took turns choosing the healthful foods. Thomas chose the part of the apple but then insisted that it be changed to grapes. He had seen a really cool grapes costume in a catalog, and he was sure his mother would order it for him.

Miss G. did say our parents could help us with our costumes. I guess that's a form of helping if your parents order a costume from a catalog for you, but I was sure my grandma would help me make one that was just as special.

When there were only two parts remaining, Matthew chose the granola, and I got the one that was left. I, Annie Pitts, was the artichoke.

5

Too Many Cooks

The Cook and the Magic Kettle is about a cook who finds a magic pot that gives her whatever food she wishes for. At first the cook wants only sweets. Each time she wishes for one, a kid dressed up as a junk food pops up out of the pot and says his lines. Then the cook pretends to eat him.

Of course, all that bad food makes the cook sick, so she wishes for good foods like vegetables and dairy products. After she eats them, she becomes healthy again. In our grand finale, we sing a song about the joys of a healthy body.

Since Marsha got the part of the cook, she acted as

if she were the queen of Sheba. She would refer to me as "that vegetable." She would whine to Miss G., "Does 'that vegetable' have to stand in front of me? No one can see me." Or she would say things like "Does 'that vegetable' have to say her lines so loud? No one can hear me."

I had to listen to this every day when we rehearsed at recess. But mostly I stood around and watched, because the artichoke didn't really have much to say. My lines were:

> *Eat your veggies every day.*
> *They're full of fiber and vitamin A.*

That was it.

After a couple of days, I knew everyone else's part, too. When Thomas was sick on Thursday, I filled in for him during the rehearsal. When Patty was absent on Friday, Miss G. asked me to say her lines also.

I was so good at remembering everyone's lines that Miss G. said, "Annie, you can fill in during the play for anyone who's absent. Do you mind?"

"No problem," I answered. The truth was, any part was better than the artichoke. Except maybe for Jamie's part. He was the fish.

Meanwhile, I watched Marsha very carefully for any signs of a cold or the flu. I would be ready! Every now and then I would walk up to her and say, "You look pale, Marsha. Are you sure you're feeling okay?

29

Maybe you should see the nurse." After lunch I would say things like "Didn't that tuna fish sandwich make your stomach upset, Marsha? I ate tuna fish just like that last week, and it made me throw up."

But Marsha paid no attention to me. She went right on being healthy. But I still watched. And waited.

A week before the play, Grandma helped me with my costume. Mom bought an artichoke so that we could see how it was put together. I thought it was put together rather strangely. It didn't really look like food but more like a cactus plant. I wondered what would have made someone think that it was edible. I mean, did a caveman accidentally put one in his mouth and say, "Food," and from then on people knew that they could eat artichokes?

These mind-boggling ideas didn't bother Grandma. She just started right in on the costume. I helped her cut giant leaves out of green felt. Then we sewed them onto my Halloween pumpkin costume that she had made for me last year. It was just the right shape for an artichoke, too.

I stood in front of the big mirror in my mother's room with the costume on. I was a pretty cute artichoke, if I do say so myself! I turned around slowly, trying to see myself as the audience would. If I had to be an artichoke, I was going to be the best one I could be! I practiced smiling and bowing. Bowing took

more practice, because it wasn't easy to bend from inside a big, puffy vegetable.

I practiced my lines over and over:

> *"Eat your veggies every day.*
> *They're full of fiber and vitamin A."*

I practiced each word as loudly and as clearly as I could. I shouted out loud, "*Fiber, fiber, fiber!*"

Mom came running into the room, screaming, "Oh, my God! Where's the fire?"

"Not 'fire,'" I said. "'Fiber.' Veggies are full of it." I guess I needed to work more on my pronunciation.

That night Mom cooked the artichoke. The real one, not the costume. But of course I didn't eat it.

6

Play Time!

Mom arranged to take off from work on the afternoon of the play. I was glad, because she doesn't get to visit my school very often like some of the mothers who don't work. Grandma was coming, too.

My father lives a zillion miles away, so I didn't even ask him. Anyway, he was probably busy with his new girlfriend, Natasha. Once I talked with her on the phone. She said, "Ello, dahlink. Pliz wisit." Mom promised that I could "wisit" next year, when I was older and could go on a plane by myself.

When I got to school, I hung up my costume and took a quick look to see who was absent. Marsha showed up. Looking well, I might add. But Jamie was home sick. Great. Besides being the artichoke, I would have the honor of playing the part of the fish.

I didn't even have to look at Matthew to know what he was thinking. He said it out loud. "Hey, Fish-face. You should be really good at playing the fish. You won't even have to act!"

But I wasn't going to let anything spoil my acting career today, not even Matthew. I tossed my hair and said, "You're such a child, Matthew." Then I turned and left in my most actresslike way. No, Matthew was no longer a bother. I had more important things to do. I was Annie Pitts, artichoke—and fish.

After lunch we got into our costumes and waited in the classroom while the rest of the school and the parents filled the auditorium. We were unusually quiet. Even Matthew. If I didn't know better, I would say that he was nervous.

Miss G. stood in the front of the room wearing a new dress she probably had bought just for the play. It made her look thinner. In fact, she had lost a lot of weight these past few weeks. We were very proud of her. It must have been hard for her to work with talking food every day at rehearsal!

When she had our attention, she spoke. "Boys and girls. You've worked very hard together these past weeks. I think this will be the best play the third grade has ever done! Now, let's move quietly to the stage, just like we practiced." I could tell that she was proud of us.

We marched down the hall as quietly as we could. It was hard because some of the costumes made swishing and clacking noises when we walked. I carried the large cardboard fish that Jamie had made. The good thing was that I was able to hold the fish in front of me when I said Jamie's lines, and I didn't have to change into a different costume.

When we got to the stage, the curtain was closed and we took our places. Marsha-Miss-Aren't-I-Lucky-to-Be-the-Star-of-the-School-Play was standing next to the big cardboard kettle on the left side of the stage, right next to the back curtain.

As she "wishes" for food, each one of the kids is supposed to sneak around behind the back curtain and pop up from behind the pot to say his lines. Then each one lines up neatly across the center of the stage in preparation for the grand finale.

Miss G. gave the signal and the front curtain opened. Marsha-the-Worst-Actress-in-the-World strolled across the stage and pretended to find the humongous kettle in the middle of the woods. She read the note attached to it:

"Be it sweet, or be it meat;
whatever you wish, you'll get to eat."

After she wished for some chocolate, a giant candy bar popped out of the pot. Elan said his part, then walked to his place to start the line of foods.

One by one, the rest of the junk foods popped out of the pot after the cook wished for them, and the audience applauded after each speech. So far, so good.

The Twinkie was the last junk food the cook wished for. Susan was dressed in her yellow ballet tights and leotards, and had a piece of plastic wrapped around her. She looked just like a real package of Twinkies, because she had even written the ingredients on the back and drawn the price and label on the front. She popped up and said:

> "Sugar is good, and sugar is sweet;
> but before you know it, you'll have no teeth."

Marsha pretended to take a bite out of the Twinkie and said, "Yum." After she was "eaten," the Twinkie took the most elegant bow I'd ever seen. Then she twirled and twirled across the stage to her place in line.

That wasn't the way we rehearsed it, but Susan has been taking ballet lessons since she was four. I guess she just automatically twirls and bows when she gets in front of an audience. The audience applauded loudly. When they quieted down, Marsha said her lines. She held her stomach and shouted:

> "That's enough of this bad food!
> I need a meal that's healthy and good."

My turn—I mean, Jamie's turn—was next. I held the fish in front of me and popped up from behind the pot. I said his lines perfectly:

"Protein makes your muscles strong.
I'm brain food, too, so I can't be wrong."

I walked across the stage, peeking out from behind the fish so that everyone would know that it was me, not Jamie. When the audience applauded, they applauded for Annie Pitts, so of course I took an elegant bow, just as Susan had done. I can't describe the feeling I had as I bowed again and again. And again. Maybe next time I'd try spinning, too.

7

The Grand Finale

I ducked behind the curtain and circled around behind the stage so that I could pop up again as the artichoke. Before I left, I couldn't help noticing the video camera that was standing in the center aisle. Our show was being taped! I was going to be in a movie!

I got so excited that I bumped into Miss G. behind the curtain. "There's a video camera out there," I said in a loud whisper.

"I know," she whispered back. "The principal said he would make copies of the play for parents who wanted to buy one. Now, hurry back in line." She scooted me behind Matthew. It was almost his turn.

"They're taping the play," I whispered to him. "We're going to be in a movie! Isn't that exciting?"

Matthew wasn't excited. Matthew wasn't even moving. Marsha motioned for him to come out from behind the curtain when it was his turn, but he just wouldn't budge. "I forgot my lines!" he squeaked.

I didn't want Matthew to ruin the play, so I said, "Don't worry, I'll whisper them to you. Now, get behind the kettle!" That seemed to do the trick, because Matthew slowly made his way over to the pot.

Unfortunately, he couldn't bend very well in the granola box. He had trouble hiding behind the pot. His head was still sticking up when Marsha was supposed to say her lines. Instead of her lines, she said, "Get down, Matthew. Everyone can see you!"

There were some giggles from the audience, but Matthew still couldn't bend low enough.

It was Marsha who took matters into her own hands. She pressed down on Matthew's shoulders, hoping to bend the box. Instead, Matthew lost his balance and fell over backward, taking the cardboard kettle with him. He landed flat on his back and was stuck there, like an upside-down turtle.

But the fall must have jolted his memory, because it was at this awkward moment that Matthew suddenly remembered his lines. And from the fallen granola box, we heard:

"Grains like wheat and corn and rice
stand tall and straight and taste so nice."

The audience was roaring with laughter by now, especially the older kids. The teachers couldn't quiet them. I really felt sorry for Matthew. I'm sure his parents were out there watching.

Other than Marsha, I was the one standing the closest to him. I marched very matter-of-factly over to Matthew and helped him get up. Then I helped Marsha set the kettle back up. In the middle of the laughter, some kids started applauding, so I bowed politely once and returned to my place behind the curtain.

The artichoke was the last one to go on, and I think everyone, especially Marsha, couldn't wait for the play to end. She really wasn't handling this very well. As for me, I thought it was fun. I was looking forward to my big moment.

I popped up from behind the kettle, but before I spoke, I gave one of my biggest smiles. I was so glad I spent all that time practicing. As I smiled, I looked at all the faces to see if I could see Mom and Grandma. I couldn't find them, but I did see someone I knew right down in the front row. It was Hank! He must have been interested in my acting after all. This was so exciting!

I cleared my throat and said loudly:

"Eat your veggies every day.
They're full of fire and vitamin A."

Then I twirled and twirled to the front of the stage just like Susan did. This was not hard at all, I decided. As I spun in front of the line of kids, I thought I heard a snicker. Then a giggle. As I spun past Thomas, I'm sure I heard him say, "She said it wrong!"

Was that possible? Could I, Annie Pitts, star of stage, say my lines wrong? I went over the words in my head as I continued to spin. I had said:

"Eat your veggies every day.
They're full of fire and vitamin A."

Fire? I said *fire*? At that very instant, I realized my mistake. At that very instant, I also spun right into Matthew; knocking him into Thomas, the bunch of grapes; who of course fell on top of Ayuko, the milk bottle; who then rammed into Gregory, the blob of spaghetti; squishing him into Max, the egg; making him tip over Maria, the banana. It continued like this right on down the line.

Pinned under Matthew, I couldn't get up; but I could see everyone fall one by one, just like dominoes, only in slow motion. There was no sound from the audience or from the stage, except for the occasional "oompf" or "ouch."

The Cook
and the
Magic Kettle

GRAND
FINA

CHOCOLATE

When the final chocolate bar had fallen, the only one left standing was Marsha-Miss-Do-the-Right-Thing. She was holding the sign that said GRAND FINALE just like she was supposed to do. The last thing we heard was the audience laughing and Miss G. yelling, "Curtain, curtain!"

When the front curtain closed, we all struggled to get up for the final song. This took a while, but the audience was laughing and clapping the whole time. I never felt so humiliated in my entire life. I, Annie Pitts, had ruined the play.

And here I was standing next to, of all people, Matthew. I didn't want to hear what he had to say about my performance. Whatever it was, I deserved it. But he surprised me when he whispered, "Wasn't that awesome—everyone crashing all over the place? Annie, you were great!"

I didn't agree with him, but I thought that was a compliment, so I said, "Thanks." I also think I heard him call me Annie, not Fish-face, so I said "Thanks" again. Maybe my Matthew problem was finally over.

When we were somewhat in order, Miss G. stood in the center of the line. The curtain opened, and we sang our grand finale. We sang about bones and blood and muscles and teeth. It was a gross song, actually, but there we were, singing our little hearts out. Well, if the show must go on, then I would go with it. I sang every verse without a single mistake.

46

When the song was over, we all bowed. Except for Matthew. He wasn't taking any chances this time. The audience cheered and clapped. Hank jumped up from his seat and handed Miss G. a bouquet of flowers. I thought that was *so* theatrical!

When the curtain finally closed, everyone marched happily off the stage. Miss G. caught up with me. She put her arm around me and said, "I want to thank you for helping Matthew. Now, that's what I call working together."

"But I messed up the play," I said.

"No you didn't, Annie," she said. "You didn't follow directions, but sometimes a surprise or two is a good thing. That's why I enjoy having you in my class." That was two compliments in one afternoon. I guess my mistake wasn't that bad after all.

Then she gave me a hug. A teacher hug is one of the best kinds, and I, Annie Pitts, got a teacher hug that afternoon.

8

Where's the Bug Juice?

After we changed out of our costumes, we met our families in the gym for refreshments. There was a table full of food with little cards attached to the plates and bowls listing the ingredients for each dish. My idea of refreshments was bug juice and Rice Krispies Treats. But Miss G. felt that nutritious treats would be more appropriate. There were cut-up vegetables, a spinach pie, all kinds of cheeses, whole wheat bread, and some things that I had never heard of before, like tabouli and couscous.

I found Mom and Grandma at the end of the table, piling the stuff onto their plates. Mom gave me a squeeze and said, "Great play, honey. You really brought the house down!"

"I guess I did, didn't I," I said, laughing.

"I hope you aren't upset," Mom continued. "I'm sure every great actress has made a mistake or two. But it shouldn't discourage you."

I knew Mom was trying to cheer me up, but I really didn't feel so bad anymore. I wasn't going to let one little mistake stop me. I was still serious about becoming a real actress. In fact, I would go right up to Hank and tell him I'd like to be in his commercial. I'd show everybody how serious I really was!

I looked around the room for any sign of Hank. I didn't see him, but I did spot Matthew heading my way. He was munching on a rice cake, and the little pieces were falling all over his shirt.

Between bites he said, "You know, this play turned out okay, but my brother and I make much better stuff. We make up stories for monster movies. Then we videotape them. He does most of the shooting, and I play the monsters. I even get to carry around a fake head sometimes. He's got some great ideas."

I was surprised to hear all this. "I thought you got stage fright," I said.

"I don't like to get up in front of a hundred people! But I think it's fun to make monster movies. Besides, you can always cut out the mistakes."

"You mean, like my little 'accident'?" I asked.

"No way! That was the best part." Matthew

laughed and pretended he was me, spinning. A rather poor imitation, I thought.

"Anyway," he continued, "my brother says we need to get some more actors. If you want, you can be the Swamp Monster, or something like that."

Matthew waited for me to say something, but I didn't know what to say. Sara and I always made up plays about brave princesses and wizards. But I guess an actress shouldn't be too fussy about what parts to play when she's just starting.

So of course I said, "Okay."

"Great!" Matthew said. "I'll tell my brother." Then he headed back to the food table.

"Such a nice young man," Grandma said after he left. "That was Matthew, wasn't it?"

"Yes, that's Matthew," I admitted.

"The same Matthew you smacked with a dead fish?"

"He asked me if I wanted to be in his monster video. I said I would. Is that okay?"

Grandma looked very serious and said, "It wouldn't involve dead fish, would it?"

"I don't think so," I answered. "Maybe just some guts and stuff."

"Sounds lovely," Grandma said. "But I've suddenly lost my appetite. Perhaps you'll finish this for me." She handed me a plate of green stuff.

"What is it?" I asked. I wasn't about to eat something that strange looking without asking.

"Artichoke hearts," she answered.

I was poking around the green stuff when Miss G. came over. "Try it, Annie," she said. "It's so delicious."

"And fresh, too," a familiar voice boomed from behind her. It was Hank. "Say, speaking of artichokes, weren't you the one who spun out of control today? Ho ho ho!" He was, of course, impressed by my performance.

"It was!" I admitted. I smiled one of my practiced smiles. I was hoping he wouldn't ask if I was also the kid who flung the flounder at Shopper's Supreme.

At this point I expected Hank to mention something about my being in a commercial, so I said, "Is there something you'd like to say?"

"Why, yes," he said.

This was it, I thought. Hank stepped to the front of the room and made the announcement: "May I have your attention please!" I didn't expect him to be so dramatic about my being chosen for his commercial, but he was, after all, an actor.

When everyone was quiet, Hank made his speech. "I'd like to remind everyone that all this food was donated by Shopper's Supreme—the only supermarket you need for all your shopping needs! Our catering and take-out departments open at seven A.M. for your convenience."

Supermarket? Why is he talking about supermarkets, I thought.

Hank turned and walked back to the food table, while I was trying to figure out what just happened.

Miss G. giggled and said, "Isn't he wonderful to do all this? I invited him to the play, and this is what he did!"

I finally realized that Hank wasn't here to see me. He was here for Miss G. "You invited him?" I asked.

"Oh yes," Miss G. said. "We've been dating ever since we met that day at the supermarket. We have so much in common. We're both interested in nutrition, and we both retire soon. Hank's already talking about the two of us opening a health spa together! We'll call it Ranch Rutabaga."

I guessed I wasn't going to be in a commercial after all. Maybe Miss G. will be in one. I can picture her and Hank together. She can hold up the yogurt and smile, while Hank announces the flavor of the week.

That was okay. I did have another offer. I would be Annie Pitts, Swamp Monster. Besides, I already had a green scaly costume. And those artichoke hearts would make terrific guts.

About the author

Diane de Groat has illustrated many books for children including *Little Rabbit's Loose Tooth* by Lucy Bate, *Bears in Paris* by Niki Tektai, *Peter's Song* by Carol P. Saul, and *Where Is Everybody?* by Eve Merriam. Her work has been exhibited at New York's Art Directors Club and Society of Illustrators. She makes her home in Chappaqua, New York.